The Time Bus

José F. Nodar

Northport Booksellers/ Spring Farm, NSW, Australia

Publisher's Note: This is a work of fiction. Names, characters, places and incidents are a product of the author's imagination. Locales and public names are sometimes used for atmospheric purposes. Any resemblance to actual people, living or dead, or to businesses, companies, events, institutions, or locales is completely coincidental.

First published in Spring Farm, NSW, Australia 2024

José F. Nodar | First Edition

ISBN 978-0-9756281-2-6 – Paperback

ISBN 978-0-9756281-3-3 – E-pub

ISBN 978-0-9756281-4-0 – Audiobook

For Miriam

Always

"Are you sure you don't want me to wait for you, Jake?" asks Jessica.

"No, Jessie, I'll be fine. You do the shopping for Milly's birthday and give me about an hour. That's all the time I need. I'll call you if I need more. It might not amount to anything, anyway."

As I reach for the door handle, Jessie asks: "Jake, what possessed you to read about this on the local paper, anyway? Since when are you interested in a caravan?"

My mind wanders back to the ad I read: *1957 Blue Bird Yellow School Bus. Mint condition. Reasonable price. Enquiry at U-Wrecks in Northport south of Western Avenue. Ask for Pauly.*

The Blue Bird Yellow bus was founded in 1932 in Fort Valley, Georgia, in the USA. How did something like that end up here?

After a successful sting as a business consultant, I retired in 2014. Suddenly, I had so much time to spend with my favourite people: my wife Jessica, sons Martin, and Ed, daughter Anna and the three wonderful grandchildren they gave us. I also had the freedom to pursue my hobbies: book collecting, writing and, of course, music. There is always music.

While doing research online one day, I chanced upon the listing for the bus and was immediately intrigued. Since I have all the time in the world, and Jessie needed to do some shopping, I figured, why not check it out? So here I am, about to see if this 'mint condition bus' really is from 1957. Mint must be in the eyes of the beholder.

"I was reading the local paper and then just glanced at the classifieds, and there it was. By the way, it is not a caravan but could be a fun caravan. We have the space out back if we decide to buy it and do a conversion."

"What is it exactly you are going to look at Jake?

"It's an American school bus, the yellow type you see in American movies and TV shows. I'm curious how it came here to Northport."

Jessie, ever-patient, gives me a smile.

"OK, Jake. Just don't buy it without discussing with me first. You bought things in the past without consulting me and it has upset me, remember? I know we have that big shed in the back ready to be filled with stuff, but now isn't the best time to accumulate junk. We've got a lot of travelling to do this year. Understood?"

What can I do? I smile and reply, "Yes dear," and step out of the car. Jessie waves to me and drives off.

As I walk to the office, I'm surprised by what I see; U-Wrecks yard in Northport is not what I expected. For being a salvage yard, it's quite neat. The place looks well-organised, with nothing out of place. The old cars are seemingly arranged by model, or by order of year, to make it easier to locate spare parts.

I walk in, and behind the counter I find a man who I presume is Pauly. "Hi, I'm Jake Fleming. We spoke on the phone concerning the yellow bus. Are you Pauly?"

Pauly, an older gentleman in his early seventies, has a solid build with a short neck and big broad shoulders. It makes him look quite menacing. His voice, however, is anything but. When he responds, it sounds like a boy talking back to me. "Hi there, Mr Fleming. Glad you made it. Still interested in looking at the bus, are we?"

"Yes I am. Before I have a look, is there anything you can tell me about it?"

"Well, sir, it is quite a story. I hope you have a couple of minutes."

"I do."

"Well then, it all started when my grandfather's father founded U-Wrecks in 1904. My father took over in 1939 right before the war. I was born in 1950 and took over the business in 1980, and at seventy-four years young, I'm still here, alive and kicking. Car manufacturing in Australia exploded in the 70s, growing to a maximum of almost half a million vehicles, and the business grew with it. Back then, Australia was best known for the design and production of large muscle cars like the Murano and other large sized passenger vehicles. More cars meant more road accidents and more repairs, and the business kept growing as manufacturing stayed strong. Hell, in 2004, Australia was still manufacturing over 400,000 cars. So here we are. Questions?"

"Not really." I try not to show it, but I'm a bit annoyed; I didn't ask for the entire history of Pauly's business. "How about the bus?" I ask.

Still, I tell myself that he's allowed to ramble, being as old as he is. The elderly tend to reminisce about the past, and you just have to listen politely.

"The bus, of course! That's where the story gets really crazy. My father told it to me one evening when I was 17. He said a tall, bearded man walked into the yard in 1967 after parking the Blue Bird outside. My father went out, saw it, and fell in love with it. He couldn't use it himself, but he thought he might be able to sell it as a side hustle. He asked the strange man how much and the man said it was $100."

"Really? A hundred?"

"Yes, sir. That is what he said. But there were two conditions for the sale. First, the subsequent sale of the Blue Bird could only occur if the person wishing to buy it inserted the key in the ignition and the bus started. Otherwise, no sale."

I don't say anything, but that seems a bit odd. Anyone can put a key in the ignition.

"And the second condition?"

"The price would only rise ten dollars a year until sold."

I have to stop and do the math in my head: from 1967 to this year, 2024, the price should be $670, assuming the original price of $100 and 57 years of a $10 a year increase.

"That's the strangest proposition I ever heard. So, your father agreed?"

"Indeed, he did. He always said he thought the old man seemed a bit spaced out, being in his 60s and looking like he was in the drug scene. He figured he would go ahead with the deal, not worry about the conditions, and make a killing selling the bus for a lot more than he bought it."

"Then what happened?"

Pauly looks apprehensive, but after a moment, he continues. "Well, Mr Fleming, according to my father, the bearded man must have read my father's mind, for he took his hand and looked straight into his eyes and my dad just froze."

"What do you mean, he just froze?"

"Exactly what I just said. He froze as if in a trance. When he snapped out of it, he immediately gave the man the $100 and had the paperwork made out. Then the man signed it and walked away. Since 1967, my dad's been trying to sell the bus, a task he passed down to me. But no one's ever been able to start it, so, like I said in the ad, it's in mint condition. No one's ever used it."

"That's quite the story, Pauly. So let me ask you. What is the price today?" I ask, though I know the answer.

"$670." Hearing it out loud, I still find it hard to believe.

"You're not just pulling my leg here?"

"No sir. If you can start it, you can take it for $670, as advertised. You also get the envelope that goes with it."

"Envelope? What envelope?"

"My apologies, Mr Fleming. I forgot to mention, there's an envelope which is part of the sale. It has instructions for the new owner."

"What's in it?"

"No idea. My father said never to open it, so I never did."

This small mission to satisfy my curiosity has turned out to be quite an interesting afternoon. I look at my watch and decide I best give Jessie a ring and tell her to take a little longer. I'm going to need more time.

"I need to step out for a moment for a quick call," I say to Pauly.

Taking out my mobile, I dial Jessie and after several rings, she picks up. "Are you done already? I am still shopping and might need another hour or so."

"No Jessie, as a matter of fact, I was just learning the history of the bus and need a bit more time, so it seems you'll be able to take that hour or so, and I'll do the same. Is it OK with you?"

"Sure, but remember Jake, don't do anything crazy before speaking with me, OK?"

"Of course, sweetie. I'll ring if I have something to share."

After I finish talking with Jessie, I come back in and ask Pauly one question. "Pauly, what do you make of all of this, anyway? How many people have tried buying the bus?"

"We've had several hundred people try to start it, but as you can see, no one's ever been successful. Even I can't do it. It's a good thing we parked it in a shed by itself, otherwise it might not be in mint condition. What with the weather and all."

"Don't you find that strange?"

"Indeed, I do sir. I could have the darn thing towed out and crushed, but it's such a beautiful machine. Do you know much about the Blue Bird?"

"Just what I've seen in the movies and TV shows."

"Then let me give you a bit more of background. The Blue Bird Body Company was founded in 1932 in Fort Valley, Georgia. The founder, Albert L. Luce, grew the company to be one of the largest manufacturers of buses in the US, and his sons carried on his legacy. Australia doesn't use Blue Bird buses, but they're extremely popular and profitable in the US. Blue Bird is now owned by a private equity company."

"Did the bearded man say how he got it here?"

"No, he did not. My father said he took the money, signed the transfer paperwork, and left. He never saw him again."

"Did you ever find out the old man's name?"

"Yes, and no. All you can make out from the worn signature is 'Me**in E**ys'. Remember, it is 57 years old."

"You know Pauly. This is quite a story. A lot to take in too. I'm surprised you stuck to the $670 price since the seller's long gone."

Pauly takes a moment to consider his response. "Mr Fleming, my father instructed me to do exactly what I am doing. Going against the conditions of the agreement of sale could put our family in peril. This man literally stopped my father in his tracks like he was a statue, and my father fought in the Boer war between 1899 and 1902. He didn't frighten easy. That's enough warning for me, so I'm sticking to his agreement. If I can't sell it in my lifetime, my children will take up the torch. Maybe, one day, they'll do what I couldn't. If not, then it'll fall to their children, and their children's children, until the bus is sold. Now, do you want to see it or not?"

"Yes, I do Pauly. I do."

"Follow me then."

Pauly leads me out the door before locking it behind us and points towards the end of the hill. "There. It's just a bit of a walk to the shed."

We walk in silence, and all I can do is look around at the stacks of old crumpled cars and commercial trucks clearly involved in accidents and now waiting for someone else to salvage them. What a business. From misery, you make money.

Pauly leads me to the right as he waves at a couple of his workers stacking more flat cars.

"Hi Jono, hi Walter," he says as they wave back at him.

Finally, we reach the shiny shed. It looks to be eight or nine metres high and 15 metres wide, and easily 20 metres deep. It's a nice big shed indeed. Similar to the one we have behind our house. I can see why they kept the Blue Bird bus here all these years. It must fit very comfortably.

Pauly opens the front door and walks in. He turns on a light switch as I join him, and there it stands: the yellow bus, in mint condition just like he said.

"Wow," is all I can say aloud as I stare at it.

A 1957 Blue Bird school bus painted in the traditional "school bus yellow"; a colour specifically chosen for its high visibility. Over time and under normal circumstances, the yellow might have faded slightly, giving it a more vintage look, but in this case, it's like the Yanks say: 'brand spanking new'.

The bus has a rounded, streamlined body featuring a prominent, rounded nose with a large, chrome grille and circular headlights at the front. Add to it are the large, rectangular windows along both sides, each with a black frame. The Blue Bird logo is displayed above the grille on the front of the bus.

There is a single door at the front on the passenger side for entry and exit. The door is typically a folding or sliding type, manually operated. Now it stands open, as if frozen in time, waiting for its owner.

The bus has large, sturdy wheels with thick tyres designed to manage various road conditions and look brand new. The rims are silver and shining brightly now that Pauly has opened the shed door, and the sunlight is beaming in on them.

As I walk around the bus, I notice a visible exhaust pipe that extends from the rear of the bus, indicative of the diesel engines commonly used during that period. Normally you see soot, but this pipe was immaculate, as if it really has never been driven before.

Overall, the bus exudes a nostalgic charm, reflecting the design aesthetics and functionality of the era.

"A beauty, right? This is as big as Blue Bird got, probably 40 feet long. These buses came in both front-engine and rear-engine pusher versions. It's pretty obvious which one this is, the grille on the front gives it away. The engine is in the front under a big cover next to the driver. They call it the *Curbside Classic.*"

I hear Pauly speaking distantly but I'm too gobsmacked to reply. I can't believe how pristine the bus looks. It's more than mint condition; it's immaculate. How? After all these years?

Usually these buses have "SCHOOL BUS" written in bold, black letters on the front and rear, with additional signage indicating the school district or bus number; however, all that is printed is one word: *Camelot.*

"Pauly, what do you think about this Camelot?"

Pauly smiles. "You're not the first person to ask about this, Mr Fleming. When I got older, I researched the word and besides the obvious references to the mystical Camelot and the presidency of John F. Kennedy it turned out there is a Camelot Public School System in a small town called Fox Valley in the central part of Georgia, with a population of 5,338. Specifically, it is in Bexar County. Fox Valley is not only home to the Camelot Public School System, but to the Camelot High School Warriors, who rank third in the AA-American gridiron football league in the state of Georgia. They won the state championship in 2017, 2019 and 2022. The area offers residents a sparse suburban feel, and most residents own their homes with median salaries in the range of $163,265 US dollars. Fox Valley enjoys many great services and amenities such as garden parks and rivers that are well-maintained by the high taxes imposed by their council area. Liberals and conservatives make up an equal share of the Fox Valley residents, and they work together to implement clever ideas for the benefit of all."

I stare at Pauly, not sure how to respond. I asked about the Camelot, and now he's telling me about the town of Fox Valley like he's reading off a Wikipedia page. He must have memory of an elephant to remember stuff like that. My confusion doesn't seem to move him, as he just keeps going.

"The public schools in Fox Valley, and in particular the Camelot Public School System, are above average with elementary students doing well in all levels and with over 83% of its high school students achieving a HOPE scholarship from the state of Georgia."

"You found all this out through the search engine?" I blurt out.

"Yes, I did. It makes for a more interesting conversation when someone asks. Don't you think?"

Feeling I should remain polite towards Pauly, I nodded but added; "Yes, but why only the name Camelot?"

Pauly just shrugs his shoulders and says: "Go on. Look inside," gesturing towards the bus.

Finally free of his lesson, I walk to the entrance only to realise that it's on the opposite side. I forgot that it's an American bus. I reorient myself and head inside.

The first thing I notice is the old, rounded steering wheel. I can't explain it, but somehow it looks as if it's just waiting for someone to place their hands on it. However, my attention is quickly drawn elsewhere as I spot the instrument panel. It looks quite modern. I was expecting 6 to 8 instrument gauges—you know, the basic stuff: speedometer, oil pressure, fuel gauge, temperature gauge, etc. This panel has well over 40 gauges and switches, some way too modern for a bus from the 50s. I see things like fog light switches, a cruise control on/off switch, panel dimmer, directional beam light switch, a range inhibit warning light, an 18-inch touchscreen and a digital radio. There are even some that I don't recognise and can't even begin to fathom what they might be used for.

"Pauly, did you change the instrument panel on this bus recently?" I ask.

"No. I do not even come inside the bus. Why?"

"The instrument panel looks way too modern. There's no way it's the original from 1957, so I'm curious who might have tinkered with it. Maybe one of your employees did some work without telling you?"

Pauly looks shocked at the suggestion and shakes his head. "No, my boys wouldn't come in here. As far as I know, no one's done anything on the bus since my father bought it. But it's funny you should mention that, because you're right—it has been changed."

"What do you mean?" I ask. This bus is getting more fascinating by the second.

"I've never ordered any improvements to the bus, and yet over the past few years, parts of it have been...updated."

"Like what?"

"For example," Pauly says, pointing to the small desk behind the driver's seat, "that small desk, those power points and USB ports weren't there back in 1967. They appeared a few years ago. Don't ask me how. Then two years ago, two desktops appeared at the back of the bus. This bus, Mr Fleming, gives me the creeps."

I let out a small snort.

"Come on Pauly, you don't believe in ghosts, do you? Mechanical and technological ones at that?"

"No, Mr Fleming, but I can't think of an explanation that makes any more sense. It flies in the face of logic."

I notice keys dangling from the ignition, as if begging me to start it. Should I? I look down at the seat. It is clean and modern, not like the old skinny seats in the buses I saw in the movies.

Instead, I look towards the rear of the bus. Even though it's dark inside, illuminated only by the glow from the fluorescent lights in the shed spilling through the windows. It's like no bus I've ever been in.

The bus interior features two rows of plush, two-seater seats arranged in seven rows. They are reminiscent of the luxurious business class seats on an A380 aircraft. Behind this seating area, there is a spacious kitchen, fully stocked with all the necessary utensils, pots, and pans a chef might need. It includes a folding table that can comfortably accommodate six people.

As I move towards the rear of the bus, I notice small screens embedded in the back of each seat, similar to those found on modern airplanes. Curious about the doors at the back, I walk towards them to investigate.

Before reaching the doors, I see the desk Pauly was referring to with the two desktop computers and several drawers. Inspecting the large bottom drawer, I notice fifteen small boxes with the same label in each: Polyglot Armlet version 7.78.

Having never heard of this Polyglot thing, I turn to Pauly and ask: "Pauly, can I open this box?

"Sure, go ahead. Just put it back where you found it when you're done."

I open one of the boxes and find an armlet. I take out the paper inside the box and read the description. My mouth drops open.

"It is a universal translation and communication device," I read out to Pauly. He doesn't hear me, so I turn back to the device, lifting it up to inspect it more closely.

It is a lightweight multifunctional device made from durable materials with a smooth and polished outer surface and a subtle matte finish to prevent glare and fingerprints. A thin, flexible OLED display wraps around the outer surface of the armlet. It's touch sensitive, allowing for easy interaction.

I try it on and find that the device is adjustable, with a discreet clasp mechanism allowing it to fit snugly on my wrist. Immediately I see that the biometric sensor detects me as a male homo sapiens and adjusts the settings accordingly and starts taking body temperature, weight, pulse and more.

"It is acting like a very, *very* advanced Fitbit," I say as if Pauly can hear me.

The screen finishes its analysis, and the small screen now starts detailing its capabilities: first, is an integrated microphone and speaker system, enabling clear voice communication connecting through Bluetooth, allowing four hands-free calls and message notifications.

Second, it starts detailing that it is equipped with advanced translation capabilities which can instantly translate spoken language in real time, but it can also make the individual you are speaking with hear you in their own language and vice versa. I wait to see how it can do that, but I get no further explanation.

Finally, the Polyglot Armlet goes through many more capabilities but the most interesting one of all is that it will never lose battery since it draws its power from the individual's breathing. So as long as the wearer is breathing the armlet will work. No charging required.

Another interesting note is that the armlet is interchangeable. Once a wearer takes it off, it loses all of their data, and someone else can strap it on, and it restarts synchronising to that individual.

A warning flashes across the small screen: *"The use of this armlet to leverage the wearer's current knowledge for personal gain will incur severe neurological pain and could ultimately lead to death. It is imperative that you do not, under any circumstances, use this armlet for personal gain knowingly. Disregarding this warning will subject you to extreme suffering and potentially fatal consequences. DO NOT KNOWINGLY USE FOR PERSONAL GAIN!"*

If this is one or Merlin's concoctions then it will go well with a time travelling bus, I think, taking off the armlet and placing it back into the small box. As I do I notice the screen going blank, before I continue to the rear of the bus.

Arriving at the first door, I discover behind it a full shower; an unexpected luxury. The second and third doors open to a toilet, providing ample facilities for all passengers. The fourth door opens to what looks like a storage rack for suitcases. It's massive, enough to fit ten to fifteen large suitcases. The next door contains a pantry, standup freezer and refrigerator, all well stocked with more than you can possibly imagine.

The final door holds a surprising sight: a closet filled with clothing and costumes from various historical eras. There are garments from the Elizabethan period, the Middle Ages, the Renaissance and more; all in different sizes and for men, women, and children. All meticulously clean, pressed, and covered in plastic, as if freshly returned from the cleaners. This arrangement reminds me of the

American style I encountered during my business trips to New York. The whole scene is bizarre and intriguing.

"Pauly, can you come back here? I have a question to ask," I raise my voice to make sure he hears me.

"There's no need, Mr Fleming." His voice sounds muffled and far-off; he's still standing right outside the door. "I have a good idea what you're going to ask. I have no idea how all that got there."

I make my way back to the driver's seat and stare at him. He's looking at the door like there's some invisible force field preventing him from entering. "Are you afraid of something, Pauly? What gives?"

"Mr Fleming. Do you recall that my father froze when the old man grabbed his hand?"

"Yes, I recall."

"What he told me I cannot repeat, but I have one word to describe the bus for you, which may answer all your questions."

"One word, eh? OK, what is this word?"

"Magic."

"Magic? What do you mean by magic?"

"Just that, Mr Fleming. My father told me this is a magical mystery bus. That is all he said, and he never spoke to me about it again. Ever!"

"Magical mystery bus? Yeah, right? It's starting to sound like you're trying to take me for a ride."

"I'm doing nothing of the sort, Mr Fleming. You're asking questions I can't possibly answer. Believe me, I've tried. Over the years, I've wondered how the tyres have never deflated, how the paint hasn't, how things appear and disappear as if to keep up with the modernisation of technology. I've had people come in to inspect it, and no one, and I mean no one, who inspects the bus has been able to start it, let alone open the engine compartment. They're just as confused as I am. There's no explanation but the supernatural!" Pauly is getting worked up now.

In any other situation, I might take it as doubling down on a lie, but he seems genuinely flummoxed by the Blue Bird. Regardless of whether it's true, he certainly believes there's something magical about this bus.

"OK Pauly, calm down. Let's see if this thing works or not before you have a coronary."

Settling into the driver's seat, I feel the soft leather sink under my weight. I wrap my fingers around the large steering wheel. As soon as I touch it, I feel a slight tingling in my hands, but nothing else. Just nerves. I reach and turn the ignition, and the bus starts as if it's a brand-new vehicle right off the assembly line.

I'll be damned, I think to myself. *It works.*

"Mr Fleming, you got it started! I thought I would never see it happen in my lifetime. Amazing, simply amazing!"

Making sure the bus is in park, I step out and stand next to Pauly, staring at the bus as the engine purrs like a contented cat. No coughing, no sputtering.

"Pauly, how come the transmission is automatic—never mind. Magic. Right?"

Pauly just nods.

Then I ask: "What type of engine does it have? Petrol or diesel?"

"No idea. Never thought of checking. It sounds almost electric, right? Not a sound, just the perfect even humming of the engine running. Strange."

"Electric? I don't think they had electric buses running in the US in 1957 or in any mass-produced electric vehicle at all on the roads back then. It just has to be something else. Any idea Pauly?"

"No sir, and I cannot venture a logic answer either."

"Can we look at it?"

Pauly, still studiously avoiding setting foot on the bus, motions for me to raise the bonnet. Before I do, I sit in the driver's seat again. I turn the ignition off and then on again, just to see if it starts, if it wasn't just a fluke.

It starts again, as smoothly as before and purrs like a kitten. I love that sound. Now I try my best to remove the cover as instructed by Pauly, but I can't manage it. There are no bolts, no screws, nothing to allow someone to open it up and get a look at the engine.

"I can't get it to open. It doesn't even look like it can," I say, defeated.

"Somehow, that doesn't surprise me. I suppose you'll have to contact the manufacturer or Google the information, Mr Fleming," Pauly replies.

I step outside next to Pauly and I stay there listening to the bus. It almost sounds like it's humming a song. In fact, the noise of the engine is quite soothing, nothing like any other massive vehicle I've ever heard.

"Don't worry Pauly. Let me turn it off and see if it restarts one last time. It might have been a couple of flukes."

Again, I plop back down in driver's seat and turn the ignition off. Waiting a minute or so, I turn the ignition key again and, once again, the bus starts. It feels comfortable. It feels *right*, like it should be at home with me and Jessie.

Oh goodness, what if I buy this thing without telling her? And if I do buy it without consulting her, how do I tell her?

I'm getting ahead of myself, of course. I try to clamp down on those thoughts and come back to the present. I haven't committed to anything yet. But again, I turn the key and the bus shuts down smoothly.

"Mr Fleming, I think you've got the touch for this bus."

"You might be right, Pauly. Do you mind if I take a moment to make a couple of calls?"

"No, of course not. I'll head back to the office. You stay here and make as many calls as you need.

As Pauly walks back to his office, and I play with some of the switches. Several lights come on inside the bus, illuminating it fully and making for quite a spectacular sight inside the shed. The bus is magnificent; there's no doubt about it.

But why did it start for me?

When I finish switching all the lights on and off, I make the call.

"Michael Peterson's Insurance. How can I direct your call?"

"Hi. Jake Fleming, calling for Michael. Is he available?"

"One moment please, while I transfer you."

After a few moments, Michael answers. "Jake, mate, how arc you? How can I help?"

"Hi, Michael, I'm interested in finding out what a 1957 Blue Bird *Curbside Classic* is worth in today's market and how much it would cost to insure it."

"Hold on, Jake. A 1957 Blue Bird *Curbside* Classic—what's that?"

"You would have seen them in American movies and TV shows. They're those long bright yellow school buses."

"Are you trying to buy one, Jake? What on earth for?"

“Well, the bus is already partly converted into a caravan; no beds but plenty of seats, a fair size kitchen, a full shower and several toilets. So, minus the beds, it would be a grand drive around Australia just stopping at hotels for a bed.”

“Have you spoken to the missus about this? Last time when you went and bought that boat, Jessica called me to bawling me out, letting you get insurance for it. I don’t want to go through that again,” Michael says, almost laughing.

Yes, Jessie might do that again, Michael, if I buy this without consulting her, I think to myself, hearing Michael.

“That’s why I am getting just a quote now, Michael. So tell me, how much is it worth and how much to insure it?”

“OK, I am not responsible if you go and do something without checking with her. Let me punch it in the computer,” he says. A moment later, I hear keystrokes in the background, and soon he comes back with an answer. “Jake, the value is around $196,000 if it’s in fair condition, and over $230,000 if it’s in good condition. To insure it would be in the $2,500 range.”

“Thanks for your help. Let me decide, and I’ll call you in a bit.”

Hanging up the phone, I take a moment to reflect.

$675 to purchase, $2,500 to insure, and well over $230,000 in value if in good condition. The bus is in mint condition and is loaded with the most modern technology

I've even seen. Maybe this bus really is magical, I think out loud.

I've been in the seat this whole time, and the longer I sit there, the more comfortable I feel—not just physically, but mentally and emotionally. It doesn't matter what happens after; I need to buy this bus now. Financially, it's a no-brainer, but more than that, I can somehow tell that it's the right thing to do.

Taking the keys out of the ignition, I walk to Pauly's office and declare: "Pauly, I'll take it. Let's get the paperwork started."

The paperwork doesn't take long, and we agree on the price. While I feel kind of bad for buying it off Pauly for $670, he's insistent, and I'm not about to pass up on this deal.

"Let me go and clear the yard a bit so you can drive it out safely, then I'll get Jono to countersign the paperwork as well. Be back in a minute or so."

While he's gone, I call Michael back and tell him to insure me. He gasps and laughs as he takes my information down, updating the system with all our polices. Michael takes my credit card details and all he says is, "It is done. You can now drive it out of the yard. You are fully insured. But I do not think safe from the missus."

While Michael was typing away all the documentation, I check the requirements in New South Wales and find out that I need an authority from Transport for NSW to drive a public passenger bus or coach that seats thirteen or more people and I tell Michael that the most people I would have in the bus at once is eleven. Michael says that the insurance policy will cover me. He just has to identify all my family members with their names, ages, and relationship. So, one less hassle and a positive to share with Jessie.

Returning Pauly says, "That does it, Mr Fleming. There's just one more thing to get for you." and goes to a back room and, after a few minutes, returns with a yellowish envelope and hands it to me. "This is the envelope that comes with the purchase, as I mentioned to you before. I imagine it has instructions for the individual who got it started, but again, my father never opened it and told me never to open it either, so I really have no idea. Whatever it is, I hope it provides you with as many answers as you have questions, Mr Fleming."

Taking the old envelope into my hand, I feel another slight tingle in my fingers. Nerves again, I presume.

"Are you going to open it now?"

"No, Pauly. I'll wait until I get home and read it then. There's no rush. It starts. I'm insured, and the drive should be easy once I get all the bells and whistles on the bus under my wing. It helps that it's an automatic."

"Yes, it is automatic, and I remember when I was seventeen or eighteen my father showing me the clutch, so how and when it converted to automatic is beyond me, but it is not my concern now Mr Fleming, it is your concern now good luck."

With that, I shake Pauly's hand, walk to the shed, get onto the bus, and start the adjusting the seat and mirrors. Then, I'm ready to start it. Again, the soft hum tells me I'm ready to go. I softly press the accelerator and head home.

The drive home is uneventful. I keep a steady pace, making sure to stay right at the speed limit—I don't want to push my luck with a new vehicle. However, there isn't a single close call or moment of discomfort. I feel completely at home on the bus, like I've been driving it my entire life. It manages so smoothly that it seems more like a sedan than a 40-foot Blue Bird.

Arriving home, I drive past the house into our expansive three-acre lot. When we first got married, we were fortunate enough to acquire this generous piece of land. It provided Jessie with space for her chickens, gave our children plenty of room to play when they were young, and now it serves as the perfect playground for our grandchildren when they come to visit.

At the back of the lot, the previous owner had built a large shed similar to Pauly's. Currently, I use it for storage, but it could easily accommodate parking the bus inside. The realisation that we have the perfect place to store the bus feels almost prophetic. So far, the sense that this bus was meant to be ours hasn't been proven wrong.

After I reverse park the bus and turning it off, I sit there for a moment, my heart beating just a little faster than normal. Then my mobile rings and I see that it's Jessie.

I pick up. "Hi honey, what's up?"

"Where are you? Still at the salvage yard?"

"No, I'm home now. Just got here."

"You did? How?"

"I took the bus home." Technically true.

"Well, that's a novelty for you. Listen, sweetie, Elizabeth has asked me to help her with some decorating, so I won't be home in time to make dinner. How about we go out to dinner tonight instead? Sound good?"

"Sure, Jessie. Anywhere in particular?"

Jessie takes a moment to think and then says: "How about you choose between the *White Sheep* or *Petite Maison?* They're both goods spots, and I can't decide."

Now it's my turn to think. Jessie is right; it's hard to choose between the two places. They both offer excellent surroundings, food, ambiance, and privacy, so I wouldn't go wrong with either. Besides, with some good food and a few glasses of vino, Jessie might not hit me over the head with the bottle for buying the bus.

"Sweetie, are you hankering for French tonight? A little vino?"

"Oh, you're leaning towards *Petite Maison*? Great choice! Let's say 7:30 PM. Meet you there?"

“It’s a date. See you soon.”

I hang up and look at the time. It’s 6 PM, plenty of time to get ready. I can even play around with the bus a little more before leaving.

As I get out of my seat, I remember the envelope. I sit back down, pull it out and open it. Inside, I find an old yellowing sheet of paper. The writing on it is smudged, but even if it wasn’t, it would be hard to read. Some parts are written in what looks to be Old or Middle English. Despite this, and the creases, rips, stains and other signs of wear and tear, the writing is still legible.

The letter begins oddly, with an illustration depicting an old carriage. It reads as follows:

In King Arthur’s era, a big wooden carriage that could transport many passengers was used. Benches or seats would be present inside, along with windows or curtains to safeguard the occupants from the weather. The carriage would feature iron-rimmed wheels and a driver seated on a raised platform at the front, directing the horses with reins. The carriage would travel on roads or paths and stop at designated places to pick up or drop off passengers. The carriage would be used for transportation, trade, or tourism...

Suddenly, I feel electricity in my hands, as if a current is running to the tips of my fingers from the letter, and the bus starts automatically—even though I took the keys out of the ignition. All the lights come on, the engine hums and suddenly a voice emits from the radio.

"Hello, Jake Fleming. I am so glad it was you who started Camelot."

I let out a high-pitched scream that I'm thankful my family isn't around to hear.

After I recover from the initial shock of the bus apparently communicating with me, I get up and look around. All the lights are on. The bus started by itself, and I'm alone but for the voice that came out of the radio. Slowly, I touch the knobs on the radio to see if it was a radio station that came on and spoke to me. Or maybe it's just a prank, something that Pauly installed before I made the purchase. Hell, maybe I fell asleep after pulling into the garage and this is all a dream!

"No, Jake, you're not dreaming. I communicated with you through this device. My understanding is that it's called a radio. I wanted to reach out before I appear before you. Let me know when you're ready to meet me."

"Who are you?"

"My name is Merlin Emrys."

"Merlin Emrys? What kind of name is...wait, you mean like *Merlin*, Merlin? The one who ran around with King Arthur, with a long white beard, white hair, pointed hat and a magic wand?" I shake my head. "That's not possible. Merlin was based on a historical 5th or 6th-century druid living in southern Scotland."

"Well, that's certainly one way I'm depicted in folklore. I'm a bit more modern these days."

"And this is real? It's not like that old American show *Candid Camera*? No one's going to jump out and tell me to smile, making me look like an idiot?"

"No Jake. It is indeed me, the one and only Merlin."

I laugh. What else can I do? This is ridiculous. He cannot be real. Right?

"Pauly, is that you doing a yarn on me? Have you installed a camera and speaker or something? Come on, mate, the joke's over. Stop this nonsense and tell me what you want."

"Jake, I am going to appear to you now. Do not panic. Just sit tight in the driver's seat. I will appear behind you, sitting where the desk is. Look now."

My face lights up in a big smile as I turn around. No one will be back there, and then Pauly's voice will blare out of the radio telling me I got pranked. It'll be funny if a tad annoying. Instead, I see a young man in his thirties dressed in khaki cargo pants and a Nautica shirt, with sunglasses on top of his head.

All he says is: "Hi, Jake. I am Merlin."

I scream again and sitting in the driver's seat gives me no way to back away from him.

He starts walking towards me and says: "Calm down, Jake. Everything is cool! Like I said, I'm Merlin. Happy to meet you," the man says as he extends his hand to me.

I stare at him in stunned silence for several seconds before reaching and taking his hand gingerly in mine. I shake it. It feels real. Warm. Strong. Young.

"I bet you have lots of questions, Jake, so shoot; let me have them."

"OK, you're Merlin, or so you say. The Merlin from King Arthur's legend, right?"

"The one and only, in the flesh, here to give you the opportunity of a lifetime with my chariot—or bus, as you call it. The Camelot."

"How is that possible? You're a *myth*. You never really existed!"

"Then how do you explain me sitting right in front of you? Cool, right?"

Doing like Pauline Hanson the Leader of the Federal Parliamentary One Nation in Australia, all I say is: "Please explain."

"Magic. I can do just about anything I wish. My magical powers are strong in all the realms in which I exist."

"Is that how the bus, your Camelot, has been able to change and keep up with modern technology over the 50-plus years it's been in that salvage yard?"

"That's correct, Jake. I parked it there, well sold it, and decided to go about exploring the world in different ways and then came up with an idea. What if I gave some fortunate soul the opportunity to travel to my Camelot and see time and space from a unique perspective? That's how I came up with this scheme. Do you like it?"

To be honest, I have no idea if I like the idea—or scheme, as Merlin called it. He calls himself *Merlin*, but all I see is a guy in khakis. The bus had been sitting in the salvage yard for decades; some guy stoned out of his mind could easily have climbed in and hidden. But then why didn't I hear him climb in and out of wherever he was hiding? How did he appear seemingly instantaneously? And how did he know my first name? Pauly just called me Mr Fleming, and I don't remember anyone using my name while I was in the bus. If this is a prank, it's an incredibly elaborate one that's clearly taken tons of time and effort to set up. It would be rude not to play along; although the more I hear from this 'Merlin', the less sure I am that he's pulling my leg.

"Look Merlin, what do you need me for? I bought the bus because I felt a connection, a pull to it. Was that your doing or is there something else going on?"

"No, Jake, you connected with Camelot and it with you, hence why the engine started, and you decided to make the purchase. Now let me tell you why it's here."

"Before you start, Merlin, one quick question. Are you an old man, or are you a young man?

I remember Pauly saying that an old man sold the bus to his father, but this guy here is not old. He couldn't have been alive back in the 60s. The man Pauly described sounded a lot more like the Merlin of storybooks, but if this guy is telling the truth, could he be the one and the same?

"I am what you see."

"OK, not sure what that means, but go ahead. Please tell me why the bus is here."

"Camelot will take you on an adventure through time and space—wherever and whenever you'd like to go. You will be able to travel and observe, interact, talk to, but you can't use your current knowledge of events for personal financial gains. All past events in the history of humankind are yours as if you were watching a movie. But you cannot go forward in time. It should be a lot of fun. Don't you think?"

"You're telling me I could see Christopher Columbus land in Cuba or Neil Armstrong land on the moon while I'm inside the...Camelot?"

I'm still not used to calling this Blue Bird bus Camelot. It feels like I'm playing into someone's joke.

"Bingo! You're a quick learner, Jake. Yes, you will be able to observe those and any other events, good or bad, but remember, you can only get financial gains. I can't stress that enough. You won't be able to intervene. So, you can speak to Christopher and say hi to him, but not tell him of any dangers lurking ahead, that's it. And in Neil's case, you can see him when he touches down on the moon, but you can't tell him what to say. You know, 'one giant step for mankind.' Understand?"

"And how the hell is this going to work? Does Camelot use *Back to the Future* rules? Am I in a DeLorean?"

"Jake, just accept it. It's magic, dude, and I'm the greatest mage there's ever been. Penn and Teller have nothing on me! Anything is possible."

I shake my head in disbelief. A random man appears in my bus, and I'm just supposed to trust what he says? That he has magical powers and my bus can travel through time and space? He's no Doc Brown—he looks more like a stoner than a mad scientist or great wizard. "It's magic" isn't exactly an answer that inspires confidence.

"This is a dream. It can't be happening. What do I tell Jessic? How do I explain the bus? She'll blow a gasket."

"Relax, Jake. Your lovely wife is going to get a kick out of this and so will your children, not to mention the grandkids. They'll have a blast, especially when you tell them that they'll be skipping school to travel through time."

The surprises just keep coming with this guy. "What, my whole family is involved?"

"Of course, Jake. Why do you think I designed the Camelot with the extra comfortable seats, kitchen, a shower, and two toilets? It's a road trip of a lifetime, baby, and you're at the wheel!"

"And if I say no to this crazy idea, what happens?"

"Nothing. I disappear, and you're stuck with the Camelot until someone else buys it from you in, say...57 years." He waggles his eyebrows. "Explain *that* to Jessie."

The man knows how to deflate a balloon. Holding onto a useless bus well into our old age won't exactly be appealing to her, no matter how I phrase it. If all this is real, there's no reason for her to get upset, but convincing her that I actually bought Merlin's bus for $670 is going to take some work. I just need to think on an approach, and Merlin can help.

"Merlin, will you be able to join me for dinner tonight at *Petite Maison* to help explain all this to my lovely wife?"

"Are you buying?"

"Yes."

"Then I'm in. What time do I meet you?"

"Let's say 8:00 PM. Just give me a few minutes to prep Jessie."

"OK dude. See you there." With that, Merlin vanishes right in front of my eyes before I tell him where. As he disappears, so do any chances of this being a prank.

Clearly, he has magical abilities, so the bus must have some as well. I'm partially relieved; I thought this was either the biggest prank in human history, or I was going crazy. I'm now 99% certain it's neither, although you never know. But now I have another problem: how am I going to pitch Merlin's plan to my wife?

With his abrupt disappearing act, I presume Merlin knows where *Petite Maison* is, so I focus on getting ready for the night. Still sitting in the driver's seat, I call and make a reservation for three. Then I'll go to the house and change clothes, call an Uber and get there early to have a potent drink of something to garner courage for the evening.

Arriving a bit after 7 PM, I spot Marta with a big smile on her face, waiting to let her customers in.

"*Ah, bonsoir monsieur Fleming. Comment vas-tu la soirée*?"

"*Très bien Mme Marta. J'espère que mon Français s'améliore*?"

"It is, indeed, monsieur. As you requested, I have a table for three ready for you. Follow me, please."

Marta sits me down, hands me the menu and offers to take my drink order.

"I'm looking for something strong but unique. What would you recommend, Marta?"

"How about El Presidente? It is a classic rum drink comprising 1½ oz. Havana Club white rum, 1½ oz. Dolin Vermouth Blanc, 1 bar spoon of Grand Marnier, topped off with ½ a bar spoon of real grenadine. It has a smooth but strong kick to it."

"Tonight, I'm game. Let's try it. In the meantime, I'll look over the menu."

"Please do. Timothée has a few specials for this evening which you may find enticing. I will be back with your drink shortly."

The menu at *Petite Maison* is always interesting, and Marta's and Timothée's specials are always a delight. I'm excited to see what might be in the cards for tonight, but first I wait for my courage drink to arrive and as I do, one of the most interesting characters in Northport walks in.

Albert Matthew Guzman: former owner of the foremost hair salon in all of Sydney, *Cut Me Crazy*, and co-owner of the hot, newly established hair salon *Locked & Loaded.* Albert and his business partner Danny Monk, who owns *Village Books & Stuff*, are well-respected business owners in the community. They have interest in several other establishments in the Northport area, including *Petite Maison*.

Albert sees me and stops by. "Darling Jake, so nice to see you. Will Jessie be here tonight or are you having a boy's night out by yourself?"

"Hi Albert. Yes, Jessie will be joining me shortly and so will another gentleman. Are you here by yourself?"

"No, sweetie. I'm meeting Danny for a bite and a little conversation. You know Danny, right? Such a darling. He is still confused over what happen with Alessia since she never answered when he 'popped the question'," Albert says making air quotes. "Alas, kids these days—what do they know?"

I'm not privy to what the question was, but judging by Albert's intonation, it might have been regarding matrimony, or an investment and it did not go well for Mr Monk. We talk for a little while longer and then he heads over to his table. Shortly after he leaves, Marta comes back with my drink.

"Here is your Presidente, Mr Fleming."

"Thanks Marta." She nods and walks away briskly, ever efficient. I take a sip of the drink. She was right; it has a kick to it, but it's so smooth at the same time. The perfect vehicle for liquid courage. Around me, the place is filling, and I glance at my watch: 7:30 PM. Like clockwork, I hear the door open and look up to see Jessie walk in.

In the time since she left meat the car yard, she's bought herself a new outfit for tonight that makes my heart skip a beat. She looks incredible in that solid high collar 3/4 sleeve loose green jumpsuit, walking confidently with the casual style of a model. Goodness, she's beautiful. How lucky can one guy be?

I stand to greet her, and we share a kiss.

"Hi, Jake. Waiting long?"

"No, Jessie. Never for you. Please sit. A drink?"

"How about some wine?"

I call for Marta and ask her to bring us the bottle of 2012 Giaconda Nebbiolo I saw on the wine list earlier.

"Excellent choice. I will bring it right away with two glasses, Mr Fleming."

"We're really splurging tonight, aren't we? What's the occasion?"

"Do I need a reason to spend a nice night with my wife? Come on, let's have a fun meal. I wonder what the specials are tonight"

Jessie just smiles. I hope I can spring the Merlin issue to her in a way that doesn't blow up in my face. Hopefully, when he shows up, he'll help my case rather than hurt it.

"Mr and Mrs Fleming, how nice to see you."

We look up and there stands Mr Danny Monk looking dapper but with a somewhat sad face.

"Mr Monk, nice to see you," I say, standing and extending my hand.

"Mrs Fleming, your husband has told me so much about you. I am so grateful for how much he supports my bookstore," Danny Monk says.

"Please, call me Jessie," my wife replies. "And it's me who should be grateful to you, Mr Monk. You know so much about local authors and have so many fantastic recommendations! Just recently, you recommended Jake *The Universe Between Us* and *Mending Hearts at Crystal Cove* by local Australian author J. F. Nodar and he has not stopped raving about them. I will have to add them to my extensive reading list."

"Yes, I make it a point to learn as much as possible about local authors so I can make the best recommendations to my clients," Danny explains. "Anyway, it's a pleasure to meet you. I'd love to talk more, but Albert's waiting for me at our table, and he's not the most patient diner in the world," Danny adds with a chuckle, a welcome change from the sadness that had clouded his face when he first walked in.

"Of course! Enjoy your meal," Jessie says.

Danny's passion for local literature is evident, and it has always been clear to me that he takes immense pride in his work. He gives us a final friendly nod before heading over to join Albert, who is already looking at his watch. It's good to see Danny in better spirits, even if just for a moment, as he walks away with a smile.

Jessie and I talk about her shopping for Milly's birthday while we wait, and Jessie explains the added decorating ideas she has for our granddaughter's room. As I listen, I try my best not to mention the magic bus and Merlin.

Just when I've run out of ways to dance around my strange purchase and Merlin's proposal, Marta arrives with our bottle, opens it, pours our glasses, and lets us know tonight's specialties.

"Tonight, Timothée recommends we start with a small mushroom risotto followed with a cold-pressed tomato soup. Then a fromage blanc and profiteroles. Since all these plates are petite, I suggest you try the Petits Pois a la Francaise with sliced Norwegian salmon as well. Just when you think you are full, I will present to you poached snapper with smoked baby potatoes and caviar. Then, a small desert of roasted apple ravioli with star anise and white pepper and, to finish, goat's cheese wrapped in puff pastry. Of course, we will complement each dish with wine and top it off with one of my favourites after-dinner drinks, a Spanish sherry with the not-so-Spanish name of Harvey Bristol Cream. This bottle and meal will be complimentary as per Mr Monk and Mr Guzman's instructions.

I turn and look at Mr Monk and Mr Guzman and raise my glass to them and they both raise their drinks and smile back. I turn back to Jessie, and she is smiling; *Yes, the evening is going well,* I think.

Jessie looks as awed as I feel.

This is what I was hoping for; a smooth evening with my wife but Danny and Albert's offer just, well, makes it almost perfect, for it is a lovely gesture on their part. Any other night, I might protest, but this exceptional meal may just help set the stage for the exceptional adventure I'm about to propose to Jessie.

"That's a lot of food, but I think I'll manage. How about you, Jake?" Jessie says, turning to me. I agree, glancing at my watch. It's 8:00 PM, and right on cue, in walks Merlin.

For a moment, the chatter suffusing the *Petite Maison* stops, and the restaurant falls into silence.

Merlin is wearing a Tom Ford Italian-made suit with a white, unbuttoned open collar shirt. He is clean-shaven, with chiselled features. He's dressed vastly different from the khaki-wearing man I spoke to in the bus. He looks good, too good. He draws the attention of everyone in the restaurant, Jessie included. She stopped talking mid-sentence to stare at him as he approaches our table.

"Good evening, Jake. This must be your lovely wife, Mrs Fleming. My pleasure, madam," he says as he reaches for her hand and places a kiss on it.

"Oh...hi. Do I know you?"

"No, Mrs Fleming, we have not had the pleasure yet. My name is Mr M. Emrys, and I'm a new acquaintance of your husband. We just concluded a business transaction today, and he was kind enough to invite me to dinner here tonight. I hope you don't mind the intrusion."

If Jessie was flustered, she didn't look at it. Rather, she seemed fascinated with him.

"No, Mr Emrys, please sit. We were just going to order," she says.

Just then Marta walks up to our table and Merlin smiles at her. She is immediately entranced by him. She stares at him, wide-eyed, and all she can say as she hastily pulls out a chair for him is, "Please allow me."

Merlin sits and continues smiling at Marta. "Please, whatever you recommended for Mr and Mrs Fleming is fine by me. Oh, and the wine looks divine! That's a 2012 Giaconda Nebbiolo, I believe. Earthy with lingering notes of rose petals, black cherry, cold tea, and twigs. Cool on the palate with substantial deep concentrated black fruits. A bold yet beautifully classic example of the Nebbiolo variety. Excellent choice."

"*Vous connaissez votre vin monsieur. Un plaisir de vous offrir votre propre verre.*"

"*Le plaisir sera pour moi,*" answers Marta, who practically skips off to get him a glass.

"Well, I don't know about you two, but I'm starved," Merlin says with a big grin.

After some more light-hearted conversation, the servers bring us our meal, and we enjoy the various delicious dishes Timothée has created. Every bite is lovely. Merlin composes himself well; as strange a compliment as it is, he eats impeccably. He doesn't drop a single speck of food, and his fork and knife look like magic wands floating in the air as he effortlessly cut his meal into manageable bites. I have to give it to him; the man is an artist at the dinner table.

Jessica and I savour the small mushroom risotto followed by the soup. Then we devour the fromage blanc and profiteroles, followed by the Petits Pois a la Francaise with the sliced Norwegian salmon. The poached snapper with smoked baby potatoes and caviar did not stand a chance against us.

The wine is spectacular, and we order a second bottle. It makes Jessie giddy, but I don't mind that. She's having a wonderful time talking with Merlin, which is exactly what I want. The better-disposed she is towards him, the more likely it is she'll be amenable to our plan.

Merlin continues to make small talk and eat as if has a second stomach.

Timing, Jake, I tell myself as I wait for the right moment to bring the conversation to Camelot.

As if we're a tandem and synchronised twirling team Jessie and I place our forks and knives down, completely full. So full we won't take Marta's offer of the desert of roasted apple ravioli with star anise and white pepper, nor the goat's cheese wrapped in puff pastry when asked; but of course, we did leave room for the sherry.

Again, Merlin has no issue with the desert and having enjoyed so much, actually asks for a second serve of the puff pastry.

Jessie is now full. The combination of tasty food and good wine has done its job and she's in a fantastic mood. Seeing my opportunity, I am about to start my spiel about the bus...but someone interrupts.

"Looks like you had a splendid meal. I'm sorry we didn't get to talk much, but I'd love for us to get together in the future!" Albert says with Danny Monk standing beside him.

I introduce them to Merlin, who charms them all immediately, and then after a few more pleasant interchanges we say our goodbyes. As they leave, I hear Albert say, "How do they know that old man? He looks like Santa Claus, with that big bushy beard and white hair."

I have no clue what they're talking about. Merlin looks like he is in his early thirties, and he has no facial hair. I look around for a man matching Albert's description, wondering if they were talking about another table, but see no Santa Claus-lookalikes. I lean over to Merlin. Perhaps he can explain.

"Why do they think you're old?"

"You see what you want to see," Merlin replies cryptically.

Then I remember what he said to me on the bus: *I am what you see*. Maybe this is more of his magic. The old, bearded man Albert and Danny Alessia saw was the same man who sold the bus to Pauly's father.

While I try to wrap my head around all this, Jessie pipes up. "Now, Mr Emrys, how is it you know my husband, and what is this business transaction you both made today?"

"Well, Mrs Fleming, Jake and I just met today and had a great conversation, and we were able to conclude a small business transaction which will interest you and your family."

"Yes, but what transaction? And how does it impact me and my family?"

"How about I let Jake explain?" says Merlin as he sips his sherry. He gestures for me to continue, and I oblige.

Here is my decisive moment; either I get Jessie on board, or she thinks I've lost my mind.

"I met Mr Emrys at the car yard when I was looking at the school bus. He was able to confirm the information that the car yard manager, Pauly, had shared with me."

"And what kind of information did he confirm for you?"

"Well, this is where it gets tricky, dear. Do you want another sherry?"

"No, I'm fine. Get to the point, Jake. What are you trying to say?"

"The long and short of it is the bus is in mint condition. Not only it is an authentic 1957 *Curbside Classic* Blue Bird, but it has all the bells and whistles of a modern-day bus, and more. When I started it up, it purred like a brand-new vehicle out of the assembly line."

"Did you drive it?"

"I did, but here's the real kicker: I called Michael, you know, our insurance guy, and gave him all the information on the bus, and he told me that its value was well over $230,000. It hardly costs anything to insure, and Pauly sold it to me for just $670. I felt like I was stealing it from him!"

"Jake, you went and bought the bus without speaking with me? Why in the world wouldn't you talk to me beforehand?"

"I'm sorry, Jessie, but it was an opportunity I just couldn't pass up. And that's not even the most incredible thing about this bus. Before you go off on me, and for good reason, can I tell you the story I heard from Pauly and Mr Emrys?"

Jessie and I have been married for over 26 years, so I know the look on her face. It says, 'you better produce a plausible explanation, or the bus is going back to that salvage yard, and you might have to stay there as well!' Unfortunately, my explanation isn't plausible. It is, however, true, and hopefully that will be enough.

"According to Pauly, back in 1967..."

And so, I relate the story to Jessie while Merlin just sips his sherry, looking around the restaurant. Every so often he focuses his eyes on Jessie, who is sitting there watching the words spill out of my mouth. I can see her mind working overtime to take it all in.

"...basically, Mr Emrys is the one and only Merlin from King Arthur's tale, and like I said, the bus...it's magical."

Jessie just stares at me with her lips pursed, and her eyes are narrowing on me like pointed arrows. Jessie continues to look back and forth between me and Merlin so many times that I start to worry she's making herself dizzy. I consider trying to explain it again but think better of it. This is something Jessie has to work through herself.

After what seems like hours of silence, Jessie speaks.

"Oh, that is a yarn, Jake. You had me going for a while. OK, so you bought the bus. Goodness knows what it'll cost us in the long term. I'm not mad, not anymore, not after this meal, although I wish you had at least spoken to me about it. What I don't get is why you felt the need to make up this preposterous story about Mr Emrys being Merlin. You don't need to write a fantasy novel just to placate me; I'm an adult, not a little girl. You made the decision and now we both have to live with it. What's done is done, and if it's as highly valued as you say it is, I'm sure the investment will be worth it once you sell the bus. Though I will say one thing: you are in the doghouse now, Jake Fleming."

My expression falls. At least she doesn't think I'm crazy, but she also doesn't think I'm telling the truth. How am I supposed to convince her? I don't have magic powers. I don't even have the bus with me. I look to Merlin, helplessly. He's the one who put me into this situation, and I sure as hell hope he can get me out of it.

"Mrs Fleming. Would it be OK if I held your hand for a moment? It will explain everything," Merlin says.

It's as if he read my mind. I flash him a grateful smile. Jessie looks at me, and I nod and gesture for her to take Merlin's hand.

As soon as their hands meet, Jessie almost falls into a trance. Staring deeply into Merlin's eyes, it looks as if she is transported to a distant place. Her eyes glaze over and open wide with amazement at what she is sensing and seeing, but I see nothing. Merlin must be showing her some kind of vision. After a while, Jessie gently removes her hand from Merlin's and sits quietly for a moment, collecting her thoughts.

After a minute, I ask her if she's OK.

"What just happened, Jake? Did I have a dream?"

"No, Mrs Fleming," Merlin answers. "I took you to visit King Arthur. You walked around the round table with me, where King Arthur sat with his knights in hearty conversation. You had a few minutes to listen. Do you recall what you heard?"

"Yes, I do, but I can't believe it. I'm here at *Petite Maison*, not in King Arthur's time—which isn't even supposed to be real! How is that possible?"

"Magic," is all that Merlin says.

I cut in quickly. "Jessie, it's a lot to take in. How about you and I head home and have a chat? I can try to answer any questions you might have, and if I can't, we can always call up Merlin. Is that OK?" I ask Merlin, glancing at him quickly.

"Sure," says Merlin signalling to Marta for another sherry.

I look back to my wife who sighs.

"Yes, Jake, let's do that. I think the wine, the food, the sherry and the experience have been a bit much for me. And by the way, Jake Fleming, you are not forgiven for buying the bus without consulting me first."

"So how do I make this up for you?"

"You don't."

"How do we even this up, baby? Please tell me."

Jessie takes a long time to respond, but when she does, she surprises me. "How about this: if I make a big blunder that is somehow broadcasted around the world, then, *and only then,* are we even. Understood? Now, let's go home."

Well, since that is never going to happen it seems I'll be in the doghouse for a *long time.* I signal Marta to let her know we are leaving, and we head out leaving Merlin to finish up his sherry.

As we walk out of the restaurant, Jessie turns to me and says: "Oh boy, Jake, are we in for a ride?"

"Yes, sweetie we are. I still don't know how we're going to tell the kids."

"We are going to assess this bus thing right before we tell them though, right?"

"Of course, Jessie, we need to make sure we know how to work everything on the bus before we speak with them and take them with us."

As I open Jessie's passenger door, she gives me a quick kiss on the lips and remarks: "Of all the many things you have done to get us in trouble over the years, this has to be the grandest of them all and if we somehow finagle this bus into an adventure, it'll be worth it."

I smile at her and just say: "Get in the car. I am hungry; let's get home."

"Hungry, but we just ate?"

I give her a look and Jessie smiles. "Oh, I understand. We didn't get dessert." This time the kiss she gives me contains so much passion my knees buckle.

I hurry to the driver's side while she slips into her seat and start the car with trembling fingers. I shoot straight home, making sure to stay within the speed limit but burning with anticipation because my wife is indeed in a good mood tonight.

~~~

Next morning over breakfast we discuss our rather simple plan. We were going to call the kids and tell them we were going for a day trip to Dubbo to see the new zoo and will be using a caravan and staying in a caravan park as an experiment for future outings as a family. We were not lying. We do want to take the grandkids to see the zoo
~~~

sometime in the future so why not test Camelot on the road. We would be back in a day.

Jessie first calls Elizabeth with the news and Missy is super excited knowing that Nanna and Pop are going to explore the zoo in advance to take her and her cousins there later. Then Jessie calls Melody and she's delighted for little Michael who is just as excited to hear the news as his earlier cousin. Finally, we call Robert, and he proves to be a more inquisitive and keeps asking why do a double trip, first alone and then with the kids; "Wouldn't it be more economical just to do the one with the kids thus saving time and money?"

While a reasonable question, Jessie gently declines. She explains with a kind smile, "We just want some alone time."

With that, the conversation ends gracefully.

The following day, we pack our suitcases, uncertain of what we might need but ensuring to include toiletries and medications. Once ready, we make our way to the shed where Camelot, our new magical bus, was parked.

Jessie hasn't seen it yet and when I open the shed door, she is awe-struck like I was at the spotlessly shiny yellow bus.

"Jake, how is this thing going to time travel? Did Merlin tell you or is there an instruction book in the bus?"

"Honey, I have no idea. I imagine that things will somehow work but let's get in the bus and look around inside first."

I step in first, ready to switch the lights on for her, only to be surprised as they instantly light up from the front of the bus to the rear.

Jessica just says: "Wow, sensor lights are just like at the ones at home."

I nod while thinking to myself that they weren't there when I bought the bus. Merlin had again made enhancements.

Jessie heads for the kitchen to explore, opening and closing drawers while I sit in the driver's seat and look at the instrument panel more in detail and again Merlin has made changes. In addition to the basic gauges there is now a new one with a label above it: The Chrono Time Travel Navigator Screen.

The Chrono Navigator has a sleek, polished exterior; an elegant blend of metal and crystal, glowing softly with an otherworldly light. At the centre of the device is a circular touchscreen interface, surrounded by intricate engravings of ancient symbols and constellations. Luckily, it also has a start here button, so I push that.

Immediately instructions start appearing on the large screen indicating that to operate it, you start by inputting the past date and time into the touch interface. The numbers and letters glow as you touch them, ensuring precision. Once the date and time are set, a holographic display emerges above the device, showing a vivid representation of your destination era, complete with historical details and key events of that time.

Next, you specify the duration of your stay. A separate dial on the side allows you to select the exact amount of time you wish to spend in your chosen period. The holographic display updates to show a countdown timer, giving you a clear understanding of your remaining time.

Finally, you input the next location you wish to travel to. This can be done through the interface or by speaking aloud; the Chrono Navigator's advanced voice recognition technology can accurately interpret your commands. The device then displays a map of your future destination, highlighting key landmarks and points of interest.

With all parameters set, you place your hands on the steering wheel of the Camelot and drive until you achieve a speed of seventy-seven kilometres per hour and then the Chrono Navigator will emit a gentle hum and a soft light will envelope the entire vehicle. In an instant, the bus will be transported through time and space, arriving precisely where and when you intend. The Chrono Navigator ensures a smooth transition, making your journey through history and future both exciting and effortless.

Then a voice speaks out through the old fashion radio: "Please indicate your destination please?

"What did you say, Jake? I couldn't hear you with my head buried in the pantry?"

"Jess, finish up in there. I found out how to do the time travel bit. Come see."

"OK, let me finish looking...give me a couple more minutes, Jake."

As I wait for her to finish and come to the front of the bus, I start thinking of the possibilities of places to travel to.

Maybe I can start with ancient Rome, walking the cobblestone streets, and witnessing the grandeur of the Colosseum in its prime. Imagine me wearing togas and chariots blazing by. Just marvelling at the architectural wonders and soaking in the vibrant culture of an empire at its height.

Or maybe go to the medieval era, envisioning a visit to a bustling castle town. I can see myself in a knight's armour, exploring grand halls adorned with tapestries and attending a lively feast. I can just imagine the sounds of lute music and laughter filling the castle and smell the hearty medieval fare over an open fire.

Also, a chance in the Renaissance era, a period of immense artistic and intellectual awakening. I would love to see, or even *meet*, Leonardo da Vinci, or watching Michelangelo at work, and strolling through Florence's streets with Jessie by his side.

Then my mind immediately goes to the American Wild West.

"Yes, I can picture myself dressed in full cowboy regalia riding through vast, untamed landscapes," I say, fully enjoying my imagination take over. I see dusty frontier towns, saloons filled with lively conversation, and the thrill of a high-stakes poker game. The ruggedness and raw adventure of the era sends a sense of freedom and exploration through me.

I think of the Roaring Twenties, a time of jazz, flappers, and unprecedented social change. I imagine myself sitting on a piano bench in a speakeasy, sipping on a cocktail while listening to Jessie pipe out a tune, Ella Fitzgerald style.

Before I can finish my mental time travel odyssey, Jessie appears by my shoulder. "What have you got to show me?"

I ask her to sit on the driver's seat and push the Chrono Navigator start button. It repeats the instruction of its use and ends with the now familiar: "Please indicate your destination."

Jessica turns to me with mouth open and just says: "Darn it, Jake; is this for real, honey?"

"It is, sweetie; so where to?"

I can see her mind spinning with the possibilities, but I have a good hunch of what her decision will be. She did her studies at uni on classical works and art, so it's most likely that will be the era she chooses, which will suit me fine as our first trip.

She's silent for a long moment and just when I am about to ask her Jessie blurts out, "The Renaissance period in Florence. I've always wanted to see Leonardo da Vinci and Michelangelo, to witness their genius firsthand." She presses a hand to her chest, eyes wide with wonder. "The idea of being in a city buzzing with artistic and scientific innovation at such a period of unparalleled human achievement has to be the ultimate trip for me."

I smile and begin setting up our destination coordinates. "OK, Jessie; we'll go there first."

"But what do you want to do, Jake? You also have a say."

"Darling, I purchased the bus without consulting you, how about if we do what you want first, OK, and we call it even?"

Jessie looks at me with a suspicious glance. Her eyebrows are furrowed showing we are very much *not* even, and I am *not* forgiven.

"You also thought of going to the same period, didn't ya!"

I had to confess, so I did, and we both laugh.

"Are you comfortable now, Jessie? Are we ready to go?"

"I am. Are you driving, or am I?"

“My oh my, you feel like driving this large bus already, are we?

“Not really, just being cocky for you.”

Again, we laugh but we are nervous. I guess we’re both thinking things like “What happens if it works getting us there but not back?”, “What if it runs out of petrol?”, “How do we fill it up?”, “Does it take petrol?”

I never saw a tank. I couldn’t even open the engine earlier—what do we do if it breaks down?

One thing about sitting inside a magical bus with the door open and having reverse-parked it is that you can see who’s coming up the front of the shed. We both look up to find Merlin standing there, dressed like he stepped straight out of the Renaissance.

His dapper appearance is elevated by the intricate details of his attire and his infectious, broad grin. He’s wearing an expertly tailored doublet made of rich, dark velvet, adorned with intricate gold embroidery along the seams and cuffs. The doublet fits him snugly, highlighting his athletic build, and it has ornate buttons made of brass that catch the light with every movement.

Underneath, Merlin has on a crisp white linen shirt with voluminous sleeves peeks out, the ruffled cuffs extending gracefully from the doublet’s sleeves while his neckline is open, revealing a glimpse of a finely crafted lace collar.

Merlin's pants, or breeches, are made of the matching velvet, tapering down to his knees. A hallmark of Renaissance fashion they are slightly puffed at the thighs and secured with gold-accented ties.

His legs are fitted in a hose that match the doublet and breeches, emphasizing his lean, muscular legs. His feet have on a set polished leather shoes with small, elegant buckles that gleam under the light.

He stands there smiling while holding a wide-brimmed hat with a striking ostrich feather plume, tilted jauntily to one side.

And finally, around his waist, he carries a leather belt with an intricately designed buckle cinching the outfit together, with a small dagger sheathed at his side for a touch of practicality and flair.

I gesture to him to come forward and I think to myself: *Damn, I am going to dress just like that.*

"Did you see the costumes in the closet, Jessie?"

"No, I didn't get there yet. Are there women's clothes in there as well?"

"Yes sweetie, women's and children's, many costumes from many eras. This bus is prepared for anything."

"Permesso di salire sul tuo carro, signore."

"What are you saying, Merlin?

"You aren't wearing your armlet, Jake?" Merlin asks.

Jessica looks inquisitively at me, as if asking what in the world he's talking about.

"No, Merlin, I'm not wearing it and I haven't even shown Jessica the darn thing. How did you know I knew about the armlet, anyway?"

"I'm Merlin; I know many things. You should know by now and be used to it, Jake. I see you showed Mrs Fleming the Chrono Navigator and have decided on the renaissance era."

Again, I look at Merlin and I think, *Can he read minds or has he a concealed microphone on the bus?*

Anticipating me Merlin says: "No, I cannot read minds, but I have a lot of experience reading people, and besides I know Mrs Fleming studied this period at university so I deduced that it would be her first choice. Was I correct?"

Jessica nods in agreement.

"Great, then are we ready to go?"

"You're coming with us, Merlin?

"Of course, I need to make sure you know what you're doing and then you can return to your own time."

"OK, let's go. Merlin, do you mind stepping outside as I drive Camelot out and then closing the shed doors behind us while I set the Chrono Navigator to 1495. I am sure Jessica would like to see da Vinci paint the Last Supper."

"Non è un problema signore, lo farò subito."

“Darn, I need to get that armlet on as soon as possible,” I say to myself, so I ask Jessie to go to the desk and grab the one that is opened already and bring it to me. She does and I place it one my wrist and see that Jessie has one on as well.

Once the bus is out of the shed and Merlin closes the shed’s door, we head out towards the M5 and head south toward heading towards Albury to find a good stretch of highway where I can hit seventy-seven kilometres per hour and not too much traffic around not to give anyone a shock.

As I drive along the highway, I see Jessie coming towards the front the bus dressed in a stunning Renaissance outfit. She’s wearing a rich velvet gown in deep emerald-green, featuring a fitted bodice with intricate gold embroidery and puffed sleeves that taper elegantly at the wrists.

The gown flows into a full skirt that gracefully sweeps the floor. Her waist is cinched with a jewelled belt, and a delicate lace ruff encircles her neck, adding a touch of sophistication. Her hair, styled in loose waves, is partially pinned up with pearl-encrusted pins, framing her face beautifully. She exudes an air of elegance and timeless beauty, capturing the essence of the Renaissance era.

“How did you get your hair done like that sweetie?” I ask wondering how she knew how to wear it.

"I did an online search and saw a video. It was not too hard. You like?"

"The desktop worked?"

"Like a charm, Jake."

"And yes, I do like what I see. You look ravishing."

"Thank you, sweetie."

Jessie looks at Merlin and says: "I am glad we have those armlets. Now we can understand you when you speak Italian—or if anyone else does for that matter—if what I read on the screen is correct."

"It is, Mrs Fleming. You will be able to speak in any language and with the dialect of the era. No one will know you're speaking in English."

"Did you make this, Merlin?" Jessie asks.

"Let's say...I thought of it, and it magically appeared. Will that explanation do?"

"It will have too, right?"

"You're also a quick learner, Mrs Fleming."

"Merlin, a couple of quick questions before we hit the magical speed to time travel, if I may?"

"Of course, Jake, let me have them."

"I understand what happens when we get to speed and the glow takes over the bus but won't a large yellow bus in the renaissance era bring a lot of attention?

"No, because no one can see the bus but me and you two as long as you wear the armlet, which is something you must always do. If you don't wear the armlet then you cannot see it the bus, understood?"

"OK, we will need to remember that then. Second question. Once we arrive at the chosen destination, how does the bus know where we need to park or do we arrive at the destination, hit the pavement and the bus keeps going at the current speed?

"Excellent question, Jake. Once the destination and time is placed into the Chrono Navigator, it will know the particulars of the era and it will levitate itself above the location letting you select the adequate landing spot."

"OK, and how do we handle that?

Pointing to a small button Merlin adds: "Simple you engage this little button here engraved with a tiny icon depicting a bus slightly hovering above the ground. Pressing this button initiates a sequence that engages powerful electromagnetic propulsion systems beneath the vehicle. Once you press the button Jake, the vehicle smoothly descends, or lifts off the ground, hovering effortlessly about one foot above the surface or any obstacle it might encounter. The sensation is akin to floating, with a subtle hum from the propulsion system audible inside the cabin. The button's activation is accompanied by an indicator light turning green on the console, signalling that the levitation and enhanced acceleration modes are active."

"That is amazing, Merlin and how..." before I can ask Merlin answers my question.

"When you program the next destination whether it is a new period or just returning to your own, the Chrono Navigator, using the internal database in the bus system and it will know the type of road that is expected and will adjust accordingly by either remaining in levitation mode or switching to the bus's tyres."

"I have a question as well, Merlin," retorts Jessica.

"Please Mrs Fleming ask away,"

"First, call me Jessie—stop the Mrs Fleming thing. Second, let's say I get a jar of coffee from the pantry, and I drop it and it smashes all over the place. No more coffee. How do we replace it?"

"You don't have to. The pantry will replenish itself. Let me show you. Go back now Mrs—I mean Jessie—and grab the two-kilo bag of sugar. Open a window and when no car is behind us, spill the sugar onto the road. Then come back here with the empty bag. Jake, please slow down so we don't reach the time travel speed just yet."

I ease off the accelerator and watch as Jessie goes back to the pantry through my rear-view mirror. As Jessie reaches the pantry, she takes a bag of sugar out, leaving none in the pantry, and heads to one of the windows near the road. She opens it and, making sure there are no vehicles following us, she pours out the sugar and returns to the front of the bus with the empty bag.

"OK, Merlin, I did like you said. Now what?"

"Well, Jessie, the pantry should now be replenished with a new two-kilo bag of sugar. I didn't do anything. No magic on my part; the magic is done by the pantry so go back and see if the bag of sugar has been replaced."

Jessica goes back, flings open the pantry door and quickly places her right hand over her mouth as if mooting a slight shocking sound. She returns to the front of the bus and just says: "Jake, we have a pantry that will never run out."

Before I can ask anything, Merlin interjects, "Same goes for the fridge and the freezer. They will never empty, and nothing will ever spoil. Magic, baby, just pure magic. Now Jake, hit seventy-seven so we can do some time travelling."

Looking at the side mirror I see there is no one behind us and the road ahead is clear of traffic as well, so I floor it and in less than a minute the yellow school bus named Camelot hits seventy-seven kilometres per hour and is engulfed in a glow light and disappears into thin air.

The glow feels warm, almost like sunlight, but with an otherworldly quality. My body tingles, as if every cell is being gently vibrated, and at the same time a sense of weightlessness sets in, as if gravity has lost its hold on me. Suddenly there is a fleeting moment of intense pressure, like being compressed and expanded simultaneously.

Sound around me fades away, replaced by a deep, resonant hum I feel more than hear. My vision blurs, then shifts to complete darkness, creating a moment of total sensory deprivation. I feel like I'm in a dark void, drifting through an endless expanse with no end in sight. Then the glow reemerges, starting as a distant pinpoint and quickly growing to envelop me again. The sensations return in reverse order: the humming fades, pressure normalizes, and the tingling subsides.

With a sudden jolt, like waking from a dream, I see a street scene from above. I slam on the brake and put the bus in neutral.

The bus is floating above a city!

"Jake, what in the world just happen?" asks Jessie. "Are we there? Did you feel all that when the glow engulfed us?"

It takes me a moment to realise Jessie spoke to me, and I quickly turn to face her in the seat behind me. "Yes, what a different feeling! I felt it and while it had to be just a few seconds, it felt like a millennium passed through my body. Are you OK?"

"Yes, I am and you?"

"I am OK, just surprised at what I saw when we reappeared. Do you see it below us?"

Jessica stands up and leans over my shoulder and sees the same street scene as we just float in the air.

"Merlin, are you OK?" Jessie asks.

"Sure. I did not feel a thing. I am used to it. Like what you see below?"

"How is it that we are floating and not on the ground?" I had to ask.

"Must I repeat myself, Jake? The Chrono Navigator knows your destination and era so it will adjust the landing in such a way that you can slowly select a landing spot once you have gauged the situation on the ground. Take a moment to look around, enjoy the view and select a landing spot when you are ready."

I turn back around and looked out over the bonnet of the bus and surveyed the scene.

The street below is lined with multi-story buildings, showcasing ornate facades with intricate stonework, arched windows, and colourful frescoes. Some of the buildings have overhanging upper stories and balconies adorned with flowering plants.

The street itself is cobblestone, uneven and worn from constant use, with narrow alleys branching off in various directions so it makes sense that the Chrono Navigator chose to levitate above the street.

I can see nearby stalls and carts that are set up along the sides of the street, laden with goods such as fresh produce, spices, textiles, and handcrafted items and the merchants seem to be calling out to individuals passing by their hand gestures.

The street is crowded with people from all walks of life, based on their clothing. Some in fine, brightly coloured clothes; others, who I presume to be artisans and craftsmen, are in simple, practical attire, and of course you can spot the peasants in their rough, homespun garments.

Women wear long dresses with fitted bodices and flowing skirts; their hair often covered by veils or caps. Jessie will fit in perfectly in her outfit.

Men sport doublets, hose, and cloaks, with wide-brimmed hats or caps on their heads, just like the outfit Merlin has on and one I need to find and put on as well.

I see children running around and playing, chasing each other through the throng or just watching street performers working for a few coins in return. Just like the buskers I see around Northport and in the streets of Sydney.

To my left over a few streets, I see horse-drawn carriages clattering over the cobblestones, carrying what I presume to be wealthy residents of the city or visitors or merchants carrying goods for trade.

While I cannot hear the many donkeys and mules, laden with heavy packs, weaving through the crowd. Occasionally, a rider on horseback makes their way through, adding to the general commotion.

A sense of energy and movement permeates the scene, reflecting the dynamic changes and vibrant culture I expected of the Renaissance period.

I cannot wait to lower the bus and mingle. And to find Leonardo da Vinci. I turn around and look at Jessie and Merlin.

"OK, the bus is steady in neutral. I have not turned off the ignition because I surmise if I do, we drop like a rock." I look at Merlin who nods in agreement.

Good reasoning, I thought.

Looking directly at Merlin I add, "I am going to put on my outfit and when I return we can select a landing spot. Again, I believe I just steer and press the accelerator and the bus will move accordingly, correct?"

Merlin acknowledges with a nod.

I am getting good at this bus driving thing, I think to myself all cocky.

I walk back to the costume closet and select an outfit. I put it on and quickly return and sit in the driver's seat ready to land Camelot.

Before I place the bus in drive, I heard Merlin speak. *"Jake, sei pronto, ti manca qualcosa?"*

I did not understand a word he says and then realised I had forgotten my armlet. As I start to get up, Merlin places his hand on my shoulder and hands me my armlet. How he got it so fast I have no idea.

"Thanks. In my haste I forgot. This is will not happen again."

“Good because you can’t afford to if you ever want to return to the bus,” he says and looks at Jessie. Her face says *exactly* what she’s thinking: “Silly boy”.

Ready now with my armlet on I place the transmission in drive and slowly press the accelerator and start touring the city from above looking for a spot to land. It isn’t long before I find one and press the brake.

I start figuring out how to make the bus go down and again Merlin places his hand on my shoulder I look at him and see him pointing a small lever with an up/down arrow. I push it down and the bus slowly starts its descent. I look again at Merlin and indicate the reverse is how to get up and he again just smiles and states: “Quick learner, Jake, quick learner.”

We softly land in a field less than one kilometre from the city. I turn off the ignition and place the keys in my pocket.

“Well, people; now what?”

“Now we find Leonardo da Vinci. Should be easy—he is well known around here,” says Merlin with a big grin.

“And how do we get to the city? I realise it is only one kilometre or so but look at this outfit and shoes? They are not meant to be walking on this type of road, if you can call it that,” Jessie says pointing out the front wind shield at a rocky and muddy patch of dirt, and then to our shoes.

“Easy, my lady Jessie; there is a carriage and horse team waiting for us?”

"What? How?" Again, that big smile comes on Merlin's face, and I just answer for him: "Yes, I know Merlin, magic baby, just magic."

I open the bus door and step out. I help Jessie get out followed by Merlin, and in less than a minute a two-horse team pulling a decent-looking carriage pulls to a stop in front of us.

"I will take the reins, Jake. I am sure you haven't done this before, correct?" says Merlin.

"Be my guest. I will sit in the back with my lady Jessica."

Both Jessie and I get into the carriage and Merlin jumps in front, takes the reins and off we go into the city of Milan looking for Leonardo di ser Piero da Vinci.

As we arrive at the city, we begin to hear the sounds of the city and its people: animals, children screaming at play, merchants hawking their wares. We see a couple of priests walking by and Merlin stops the carriage.

I ask: *"Mi scusi, santità. sai dov'è il signor Leonardo di ser Piero da Vinci?"*

To my surprise I don't hear myself say in Italian "Excuse me your holiness. do you know where Mr Leonardo di ser Piero da Vinci is?" but the armlet worked and one of the priests answered with *"Il maestro è al refettorio di Santa Maria delle Grazie,"* or "The maestro is over at the refectory of the Santa Maria delle Grazie."

He points straight ahead and I nod, give thanks and Merlin points the horses in this direction.

We arrive and find the church, divided into a nave and two aisles, reflecting the style that was typical of Lombardy at the beginning of the Renaissance period, which featured ogival vaults and a gabled façade from its sloping roof.

Walking in we stroll around undisturbed and there in the narrower sides of the hall we find Leonardo di ser Piero da Vinci staring at the beginnings of the Last Supper.

"OK, Jessie, here is your chance. Go and chat up da Vinci for a bit. Merlin and I will just stay here."

Jessie makes sure her armlet is on tightly and walks up to Leonardo and starts the conversation: "Wow, this place is incredible! Are you...are you Leonardo da Vinci?"

A smiling Leonardo answers with: "Indeed, I am. And who might you be, my unexpected visitor?"

"My name is Jessie. I...uh...come from a place far away. I've always admired your work. Can you tell me what inspired you to create this mural?"

"The Last Supper. It is a work that holds much significance. I wanted to capture a moment of profound spiritual and emotional importance. The moment when Christ reveals that one of his disciples will betray him. Each apostle's reaction reflects the turmoil within the human soul."

"It's truly a masterpiece. The way you portrayed the emotions, the tension...it's like they come to life right in front of you. How did you manage to convey such depth?"

A thoughtful Leonardo takes a moment to answer and comes up his response: "It was not an easy task. I spent countless hours studying human expressions and movements. I wanted each gesture, each glance, to tell a story. To show the complexity of human nature and the divine."

"Yes, I see. It's amazing how you achieved that. You have such a gift for capturing the essence of your subjects. Have you ever thought about painting something more...personal?"

"Personal? What do you mean?"

"You know something like a portrait that isn't just about the physical appearance but also the inner life, the soul of the person."

Nodding slowly, he answers Jessie: "I see what you mean, yes. I have considered it. In fact, I have been contemplating a new project. A portrait that embodies not just beauty, but also mystery and depth. A face that invites the viewer to ponder, to imagine the life behind the eyes."

With a big grin Jessie adds: "That sounds incredible. I think you'd be perfect for it. Your ability to see beyond the surface, to capture the unseen, is unparalleled."

Looking at Jessie intently Leonardo continues his statement: "You have given me much to think about, Lady Jessie. Your presence here is...inspiring. There is something about you, a quality that I cannot quite define. Perhaps you might be the muse I have been searching for."

"Me? I don't know about that..." says Jessie blushing a little.

With a warm smile Leonardo adds: "You have a unique aura, Lady Jessie. If you would permit me, I would like to capture it. To paint a portrait that will transcend time."

"Oh no, kind sir, that will not be possible. I merely wondered what you've been thinking as a future project. You have been more than honest with me sharing your future projects. Thank you so much."

"Very well, though unexpected; you have sparked a new vision within me. I shall begin work on this portrait, and perhaps it will be my most significant creation yet."

"I can't wait to see it. Thank you, Leonardo."

"No, thank you, Lady Jessie. You have given me the courage to embark on this new journey. I am so grateful for this additional inspiration."

"I will leave you now and return to my companions. It has been an honour, sir."

"The honour has been mine." Leonardo bows to Jessie and she, in turn, curtsies before returning to me and Merlin.

As they walk out of the church I ask: "Well, how did it go?"

"Oh, my goodness, Jake—it was fantastic. Leonardo is gracious but has a reserved personality at the same time I could tell by his demeanour, but he presents such an elegant bearing. What a thrill!"

"What did you speak about, Jessie?" asks Merlin.

"Well, I asked him what inspired him to paint the mural, and how is he able to convey such emotion in that mural and finally what is he thinking on doing in the future."

"And his responses?"

"Basically, he just said he wanted to ensure his painting reflect the emotions, passions of the human soul."

"Yes, he is an interesting individual. Way ahead of his time with this mural and of course all his other conceptually inventions such as the parachute, the helicopter, an armoured fighting vehicle, the use of concentrated solar power, and a few others."

"Indeed, Merlin. So, what do you want to do now Jessie?" I ask.

Looking at her armlet, she touches the screen and sees that we have spent almost a day in our little adventure, and we did tell the kids we would be only away one day, so she says: "Let's go home, Jake."

I look at Merlin and he answers: "You two go ahead. You know what you are doing now. I will stay here and enjoy this era for a while. I might pop in to see you in a week or two, OK? Let's go back to the carriage and I will drop you off."

We arrive and find Camelot exactly where we left it undisturbed. Merlin drops us off and waves goodbye and heads back to Milan. Jessie and I hop inside, quickly change out of our costumes and this time, instead of manually setting the Chrono Navigator I use the voice activated command and simply say: "Home, Camelot; takes us home."

Jessie and I see the glow envelope us once again and we disappear.

I am not sure how it happened and how the Chrono Navigator knew, but somehow we ended up back inside the shed, with the shed door closed, and all in one piece.

We're home, safe and sound.

Jessie and I exit the shed, walk into the house and as we walk inside Jessie then says in a matter-of-fact way: "I am hungry. How about I cook something light, and we have it sitting at the breakfast bar and then off to bed? OK with you?"

"Sure, sweetie; what do you have in mind?"

"How about some wine, and a nice spread of antipasto? Sounds good?"

"Sure. I will get the wine and you get started making the spread. Do you mind if I turn on the TV and catch up on the news?"

"No, good idea."

"Great, let me get the wine."

While Jessie and I are not wine experts, we do like wine, and we have converted one of the smaller bedrooms into a wine cellar of sort and we have quite a good collection of wines. Some expensive but for the most part sensibly price bottles of wines from Spain, New Zealand, Germany, France and of course Australia. Our collection is about one and sixty bottles, so we have enough wine to enjoy it for a long time. I grab one of those sensibly priced wines from Spain

I look up and down and settle on a Campo Viejo Rioja Tempranillo. This wine pours a deep ruby red with hints of violet, indicative of its youth and vibrancy and should go well with the antipasto. As I reach for the bottle, I hear a loud crash, like plates crashing onto the floor, and Jessie calling out my name.

Fearing the worse I rush back to the kitchen and find several plates shattered on the kitchen floor and Jessie trembling.

I walk up to her and ask: "What is wrong, sweetie?"

Jessie does not answer, just points at the kitchen TV and there I see an announcer in front of the Louvre in

France, so I turn up the volume. What I hear is flabbergasting.

"Good evening, ladies and gentlemen. We are reporting live from the Louvre in Paris, where an astonishing and baffling event has just been confirmed. In an unprecedented twist, the world-renowned painting, the Mona Lisa, has been altered. Yes, you heard that correctly. The famous visage of Lisa Gherardini, immortalised by Leonardo da Vinci, has inexplicably changed to depict a completely different person."

Pausing for effect the announcer continues: "Museum officials have confirmed that the altered painting remains an authentic work of Leonardo da Vinci, but how this transformation occurred overnight is a mystery that has left experts and authorities completely stumped."

As Jessie and I stand in the kitchen, silent and astounded, we see a brief clips of the altered painting, showing a new, yet equally captivating face, with different features but still bearing the unmistakable touch of Leonardo's genius. Museum visitors and staff are shown reacting with shock and disbelief.

The announcer continues: "Art historians and scientists are now scrambling to understand the implications of this phenomenon. The painting's brushstrokes, pigment composition, and even the underlying sketches all confirm that this is, without a doubt, a genuine Leonardo da Vinci piece. Yet, the subject is now someone entirely different from the woman we have known and revered for centuries."

"Speculation is rife. Some suggest this could be the work of an incredibly sophisticated forgery, though experts have dismissed this theory due to the near-impossible level of skill required to replicate Leonardo's technique so perfectly. Others wonder if this might be a case of advanced technology or even a supernatural event."

"For now, the art world holds its breath as this mystery unfolds. How did this change happen? Who is the new person portrayed in the painting? And what does this mean for the legacy of Leonardo da Vinci and one of the most famous artworks in history? Stay tuned as we continue to bring you updates on this extraordinary story. Reporting live from the Louvre in Paris, I'm Amélie Moreau. Back to you in the studio."

I turn off the TV.

"Jessie, I think we might need something a bit stronger than wine. Did you see the new Mona Lisa?"

"Yes."

"Do you recognise her?"

"Yes."

"What else happened with Leonardo and your conversation with him?

Feeling a bit uncomfortable at my question Jessie hesitates a bit but finally gathers her courage and says: “He wanted me to pose for him as a personal project and of course I said no. But it seems he used me as an inspiration, a muse, and from memory he painted me and not the original person for the Mona Lisa.”

“Well, babe, I purchase Camelot without consulting you and now you changed the face of history when it comes to the Mona Lisa. I say we’re even.”

José F. Nodar

Flung into one of life's biggest challenges at just eleven, José's story began in Havana, Cuba. The Cuban revolution forced him onto a plane alone, landing him at an orphanage in a small Georgia town called Washington. Reuniting with his parents wouldn't happen until he was eighteen and a high school graduate in Atlanta.

Business Administration became his focus at Georgia State University. From there, he navigated the world of finance, first at the First National Bank of Atlanta (now Wells Fargo) and later as a project manager in financial consulting. These roles took him across the United States, Europe, and even Australia.

It was in Camden, New South Wales, Australia, that a spark ignited José's creative side. A writers' group became the launching pad for his debut novel, and soon, his mind birthed Danny Monk, his first major character.

Currently, José is a prolific writer, working on his seventh short story collection alongside a new crime novel slated for release in 2026.

But José's life isn't all about writing. When he's not crafting captivating stories, you might find him at the local mall, observing the world and gathering inspiration for future characters. Away from his computer, he dives into books or enjoys long, leisurely walks with his wife Miriam around Camden.

www.ingramcontent.com/pod-product-compliance
Lightning Source LLC
Chambersburg PA
CBHW061108100726
47911CB00012B/465
* 9 7 8 0 9 7 5 6 2 8 1 2 6 *